Prescription for Change

Also by Dr. Dorothy Wagner

PRESCRIPTION FOR LIVING
PRESCRIPTION FOR SUCCESS
PRESCRIPTION FOR HAPPINESS OVER 50

Prescription for *Change*

Dr. Dorothy Wagner

Fawcett Columbine • New York

A Fawcett Columbine Book
Published by Ballantine Books
Copyright © 1987 by Dorothy Wagner, Ph.D.

Library of Congress Catalog Card Number: 89-91779

ISBN: 0-449-90473-3

Manufactured in the United States of America

First Ballantine Books Edition: August 1990

10 9 8 7 6 5 4 3 2 1

Prescription for Change

Change is possible for all of us, if we are willing to risk it. It is never too late!

How tragic to have to say,
I only wish I had _____.

Change is scary as hell, but the alternative is to spend the rest of your life as it is now.

Everyone is afraid of change. Because of this people stay in "dead end" jobs and bad marriages.

Don't become discouraged. Change is very difficult and takes much time, but the brave ones go on to grow and succeed.

Our actions are predicated on our early life experiences and traumas.

Human beings have a need to understand and to create wholeness of their life experiences.

When this is not done, the result is an "acting out" of the early traumas and painful experiences.

"Acting out" can take the form of drinking, drugs, self-sabotaging behavior and other "clever" ways to shorten or make our lives miserable.

Can you imagine how much self-hatred a person must have to inhale or inject chemicals into their body?

Self-hatred causes us to be ill-tempered and defensive. We owe it to those we love to learn to forgive and love ourselves.

We must change our way of thinking before we can change our behavior, or we are doomed to a life of unmet expectations.

It is possible to feel great ambivalence toward our parents. Thus we can dearly love and hate them at the same time.

There are many unloving parents but few children who do not desperately want their parent's love.

As children, we are vulnerable and helpless in the face of parental abuse. It is not unlike a master/slave relationship.

Many of us remain a child in many ways, looking for the love we longed for from parents incapable of giving it to us.

You are not born with an inferiority complex. It was a 'gift' from someone whose love you sought.

People who have been rejected tend to reject others thus perpetuating their own experience.

Do you frequently ask, "Why me?"
The truth is, life is NOT fair!
You've got to make the best of it.

"If only" is a futile game and can be dangerous to your mental health.

You must learn to separate the truth (reality) from your own truth (distortion).

Narcissistic individuals must always be in control. They cannot admit to any vulnerability or imperfection.

- Don't be afraid to be human.
- Human beings make mistakes.
- Human beings are not perfect.

Learn to know yourself. Trust your instincts and you will treat others with more understanding and love.

Look around you, see all the angry people. It is easier to express anger than pain.

Keep contact with cold, rigid people to the absolute minimum.

Two-thirds of all the hospital beds in this country are now occupied by mental patients. Mental illness is caused by an excess of guilt and anger.

The extreme manifestation of guilt is seen in people who tend to hurt themselves physically or confess to crimes they did not commit.

The victim of a guilt-complex probably acquired it at an age when true guilt was not possible.

Others never defeat you. You defeat yourself in an attempt to punish yourself because of feelings of guilt.

You allow yourself only as much love, money, success, and peace of mind as your guilt can tolerate.

People only see what they are prepared
to see.

As adults, we are responsible for our experiences because we create them.

We all have much more control over our lives than we are willing to admit.

Accepting that we have control
means accepting responsibility
for our circumstances.

Self-improvement should be a
never-ending process and continue
all of our lives.

We very rarely understand our own motivation and the root causes of our own discomfort.

Not to know is bad, not to want to know could prove fatal.

Denial grows until it kills you, either physically or spiritually.

In therapy, the contents of the unconscious are explored to help the person realize the distortions in their self-perception.

Emotional wounds can cause us to dis-associate from our body. Integration can be achieved through therapy.

Separation of psyche (mind) and soma (body) is thought to be at the root of many physical as well as psychosomatic illnesses.

Neurosis is always a substitute for legitimate suffering.

—Carl Jung

If you close yourself off to pain, there is a generalized deadening of emotion. You have also closed yourself off to joy!

People who experience depression and anxiety are infinitely more healthy than those who repress and deny their feelings.

People are frightened by their feelings because it makes them feel too vulnerable. Be brave!

The healthy person is willing to face his problems, however painful, in the knowledge that it will improve the quality of his life.

Individual therapy, with the right therapist for you, will eventually free you of the burden of anger and guilt.

Growth is often very painful, but it leads to greater self-esteem and independence.

An individual who has gained insight sees the world in another dimension and can never deny that reality again.